HARQUIN

The Fox who went down to the Valley

Written and illustrated by

JOHN BURNINGHAM

JONATHAN CAPE, 30 BEDFORD SQUARE, LONDON

for Lucy

By the same author:
BORKA
TRUBLOFF
ABC
HUMBERT
CANNONBALL SIMP
SEASONS
MR GUMPY'S OUTING

and the John Burningham Wall Friezes:
BIRDLAND
STORYLAND
LIONLAND
JUNGLELAND
WONDERLAND

First published 1967
Reprinted 1969, 1971
Jonathan Cape Ltd, 30 Bedford Square, London WC1
ISBN 0 224 61213 1
ISBN 0 224 61213 1
Printed in Great Britain by Fletcher & Son Ltd, Norwich
Bound by Richard Clay (The Chaucer Press) Ltd, Bungay, Suffolk
Typography and title-page design by Jan Pienkowski

This is a story about Harquin the Fox. He lived with his family. Their home was at the top of a hill, and they were able to live peacefully because the local squire and his gamekeeper, who used to hunt foxes, did not know they were there.

Now Harquin's parents would often warn the young foxes. 'You can play here on the hill,' they would say, 'but don't go down to the valley, otherwise the huntsmen will see you and follow you back here and we will no longer be safe.'

But Harquin was bored with playing on top of the hill.

He would secretly go down to the valley at
night while everyone was asleep. There were
many interesting things. Harquin liked to
smell the flowers that grew in the gardens.

In the valley there were also some very
treacherous marshes which nobody dared to
cross for fear of sinking into the mud. But
Harquin discovered a secret route across them,
and on the other side he used to catch rabbits
and chickens.

One evening Harquin's father called all the
family together. 'I have reason to believe', he
said, 'that one of you has been going out at
night. Now I must warn you all again about
going down to the valley. Remember what
happened to your uncle,' he added, pointing
to the picture on the wall. 'He was caught
by the huntsmen.'

But Harquin would not listen. He used to
run through the village, making sure that he
was not seen.

One night when Harquin was returning home, he *was* seen by the gamekeeper.

Bang! Bang! went the gamekeeper's gun. The shot missed Harquin but gave him a terrible fright.

'I didn't know there were foxes living around here,' thought the gamekeeper. 'I must tell the squire about this so that he can bring the hunt here.'

Harquin's parents heard the bangs and saw Harquin rushing home. 'I warned you,' said his father. 'Now we'll all be killed when the huntsmen find us.'

'Whatever shall we do?' cried his mother.

The next day the gamekeeper went to see the squire and told him about the fox. 'Good!' said the squire. 'We'll take the hunt there on Saturday. We've never been up that valley before: I didn't know there were foxes there.'

Harquin's parents feared the next hunt would come looking for them. 'It's best that we remain here and just hope that they won't discover our home,' the parents told the little foxes.

But Harquin was making his own plans. 'I must lead the hunt away from here,' he thought.

Early on Saturday morning Harquin left and went down to the valley. He hid in some undergrowth where he was able to watch the huntsmen gathering in the village square. As soon as the master blew his horn and the hunt began to move off, Harquin rushed ahead and waited.

He waited until he was quite sure the huntsmen had seen him.

'We're not far behind him now,'
shouted the squire.

Harquin ran for his life. 'If only I can reach
the marshes in time!' he thought.

At last he reached the edge of the marsh
and sped along his secret path.

But the hounds, horses and huntsmen did
not know the way across and…

SPLOSH! SPLASH!
they all fell into the slimy mud.

The squire, who had been thrown into the marsh head-first, was furious and shook with anger. 'Call off the hounds,' he bellowed. 'We cannot hunt in this bog. The hounds can't find the scent and we shall lose them.'

The squire was so angry that he broke his riding crop. 'Where's that gamekeeper fellow who suggested this hunt?' he roared.

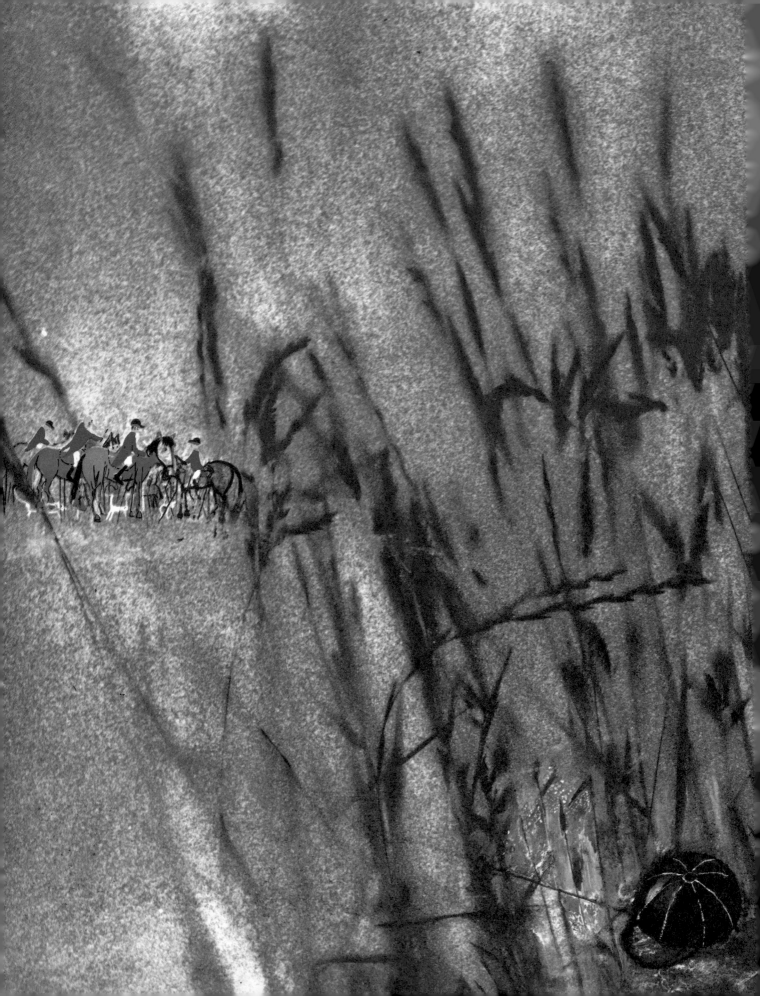

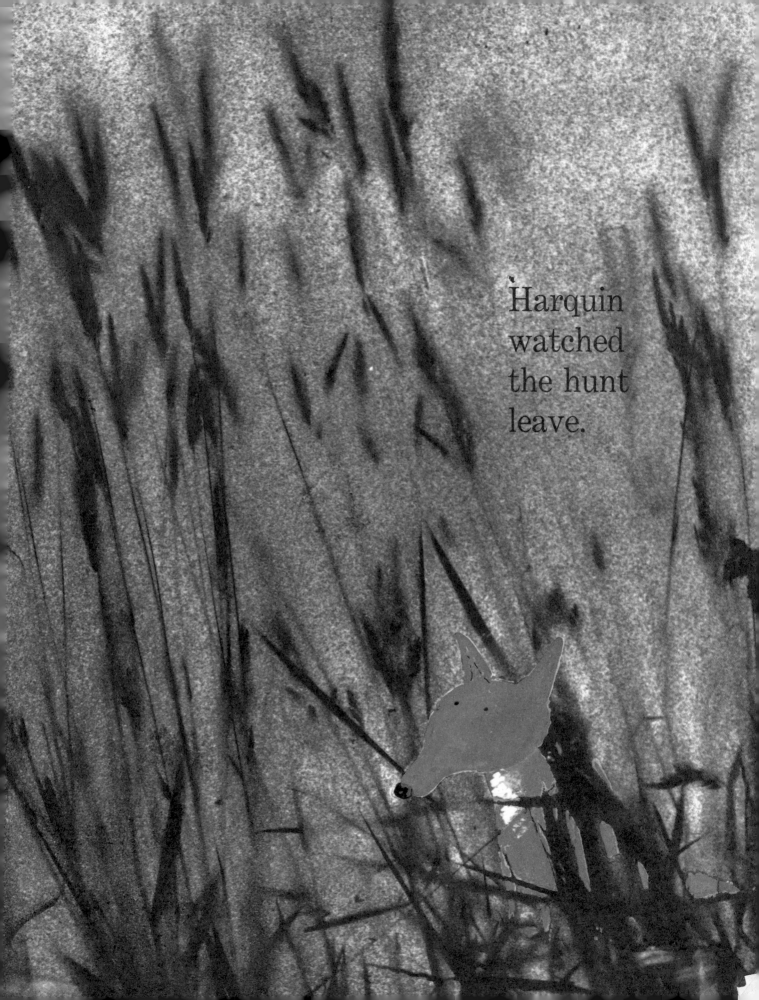

Harquin
watched
the hunt
leave.

He made quite sure they had gone before
he ventured out, taking with him, as a
souvenir, the squire's hat which he found in
the marsh. His family was very pleased to see
him returning home safe and sound, and came
out to meet him.

And so the foxes were able to live in peace
and wander freely in the valley, since nobody
ever went there to hunt again. As for the
gamekeeper, he no longer works for the
squire.

Now Harquin has children of his own and they still live in the same home. Often before they go to sleep, he tells them about the famous hunt. They all listen intently to his stories, except for one of his sons, who is bored. He wants to go beyond the valley.